Heaven

NICHOLAS ALLAN

To Isabella

HEAVEN

A RED FOX BOOK 978 0 099 48814 9 (from January 2007)

0 099 48814 0

First published in Great Britain by Hutchinson,
an imprint of Random House Children's Books

Hutchinson edition published 1996
Red Fox edition published 1998
This Red Fox edition published 2006

3 5 7 9 10 8 6 4 2

Red Fox Books are published by Random House Children's Books,
61–63 Uxbridge Road, London W5 5SA,
a division of The Random House Group Ltd,
in Australia by Random House Australia (Pty) Ltd,
20 Alfred Street, Milsons Point, Sydney, NSW 2061, Australia,
in New Zealand by Random House New Zealand Ltd,
18 Poland Road, Glenfield, Auckland 10, New Zealand,
and in South Africa by Random House (Pty) Ltd,
Isle of Houghton, Corner Boundary Road & Carse O'Gowrie, Houghton 2198, South Africa.

THE RANDOM HOUSE GROUP Limited Reg. No. 954009

www.kidsatrandomhouse.co.uk

www.nicholasallan.co.uk

A CIP catalogue record for this book is available from the British Library.

Printed in China

Early one morning Lily woke up to find
Dill the dog packing.

"Where're you going?" she asked.
"Up there," said Dill.

"Can I come too?"
"Er . . . not yet," said Dill.
"But I want you to play."
"I'll be late," said Dill.

"Late for what?"
"I'm being collected."

"Why can't I come too?"
"You have to be invited," said Dill.
"Who invited *you*?" asked Lily.

"Us . . ."

said the angels.

"Does Dill have to go *now*?" asked Lily.
"Now," said the angels.
"Can't he stay just ten minutes?"
"Well . . . five minutes," said the angels.

"Will you be away long?" asked Lily.
"A long time," said Dill.
"But you might not like it up there."
"I *will* like it up there."
"You might not though."
"Of *course* I'll like it. It's heaven, isn't it?"
"Might not."

"What do you think it's like then? Up there?"
"Nice," said Dill.
"Yes, but what's it *like*?"
"What do *you* think it's like?"

"Well," said Lily. "In heaven there's a funfair where all the rides are free and you're never sick once."

"And there's a whole island made of chocolate
with ice-cream clouds and sweets in caves and the sea
is made of Coke and you can eat all you want
AND YOU'RE NEVER SICK ONCE!"

"No, no, no, no, no," said Dill. "It's not like *that* at all."
"Well, what is it like then?"

"Bones," said Dill.
"Bones?"
"Bones. All over the place. And not just *ordinary* bones.
These have bits of meat on them, every one of them."

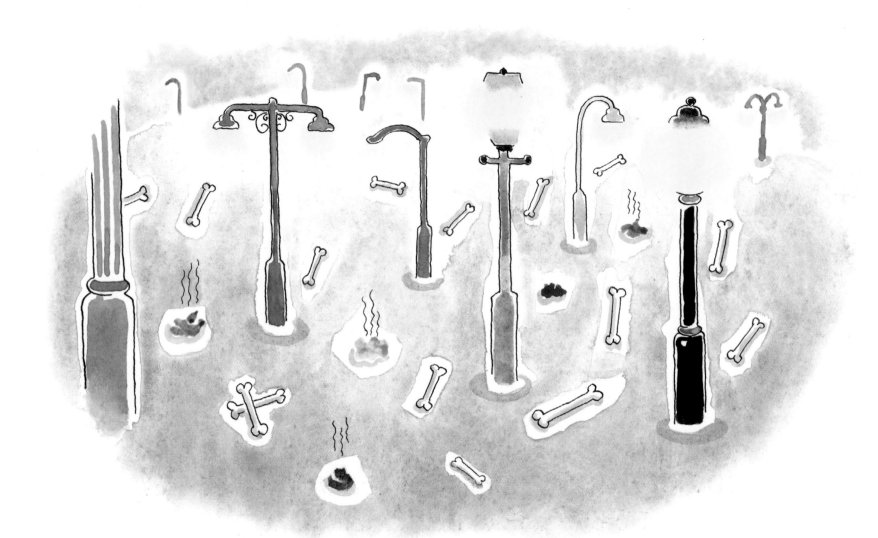

"And there are lampposts. Hundreds of them.
And whiffy things to smell on the ground."

"**YUCK!**" said Lily. "Bones, lampposts, whiffy things.
Doesn't sound like heaven to me."
"Nevertheless, that's what heaven's like."
"How do *you* know?" said Lily.
"How do you know it's not?" said Dill.

"Well, if it is, *I* wouldn't want to go there."
"Don't worry. You're not invited anyway."
"Wouldn't want to go anyway."
"Wouldn't want you there, thanks."

"Anyway, you might
not go up – you might
go **DOWN**," said Lily.
"Down?" said Dill.

"Down," said Lily.
"But I've always been a
good dog," said Dill.

"What about that time you
stole the chicken?"
"Well, apart from that," said Dill.

"What about the time you
bit Aunt Julia?"
"Well, apart from that," said Dill.

"What about the time
you . . . ?"

"All right, I've *tried*
to be a good dog. *OK?*"
"Hmmph!" said Lily.

"Time," said the angel.

Lily walked home and went back to bed.
When she woke up it was late.
She ran downstairs and saw Dill's basket . . .

and his bowl . . .

and his scratches on the door . . .

and his lead . . .

and his yucky wet tennis ball.
She was very sad.

Lily thought things would never be the same again.
But one day she met . . .

a stray puppy. She took him home,
and then began to remember all that Dill had said.

She took the puppy for a walk and
found a street full of lampposts . . .

and whiffy things . . .

and when they got home she gave him lots of bones –
all with bits of meat on them.

He must think he's in heaven already,
thought Dill.